Amma, Tell Me About Holi !

Written by
Bhakti Mathur

Illustrated by
Maulshree Somani

There once lived a little boy,
Klaka was his name.
Countless friends he had,
With whom he played many a game!

Large eyes, a wide smile,
Teeth like pearls in a row,
His brother was called Kiki,
And his golden dog, Frodo.

Every night, their Amma
Tucked Klaka and Kiki into bed,
And then it would be time
For a story to be read:

Of queens brave
And kings handsome
Of pirates cunning
And demons fearsome.

Today Klaka was excited
But the day passed slowly,
For Amma had promised,
To tell him all about Holi.

He'd been agog since morning
Waiting, waiting for bed time,
He hopped into Amma's lap
Soon as he heard the clock chime!

"My favorite festival of all", said Amma,
"Is the festival of colours we call Holi.
It's the coolest party of the year,
Celebrated with friends and family.

A day to have fun, forget all the rules
A day to be as naughty as you can be,
Fling water balloons that go splat,
And drench Kiki and Daddy and me!

Shoot with water pistols called *pichkaris*
Smear paint on and get smeared by friends,
Creep up on them, slowly from behind,
And pour a bucket of water over their heads!"

"But why colour someone?" asked Klaka
"And why let them smear and drench us?"
Amma said, "That comes from a tradition
Started long ago by Krishna the mischievous!

You see Krishna was blue like the sky
But his friend Radha was white as snow
And Krishna would often ask his Amma
"Why isn't Radha blue like me—why is it so?"

One day his Amma said to him in jest
"I really can't say why Radha isn't blue,
Why don't you throw some blue color on her
If you want her to look just like you?"

Naughty Krishna did exactly that
And the prank he played that day,
Became a tradition that we celebrate
As the beautiful festival of Holi today.

The coloured dyes of Holi
Are called *Gulaal* and *Abeer*,
Years ago, these colours were made
From the leaves of the *Palaash* tree.

Holi falls on the day of the full moon
In March, when flowers again bloom,
It marks the arrival of cheery spring
And the end of winter's cold gloom.

The night before Holi, we burn
A big bonfire of twigs and branches,
To celebrate the burning of Holika
Who was a really evil enchantress.

From Holika does Holi get its name
And it also marks the celebration.
Of all that is good in this world
And of evil's ultimate decimation.

Holika was the evil sister
Of a demon king as wicked as can be,
His name was Hiranyakashipu, and
He caused terror across the country.

He wanted everyone to worship
Only him as their divine Lord,
And mercilessly punished those
Who did not bow to him as God.

Now absolutely the opposite
Was the King's son Prahlad,
A good boy, a kindly boy
With an unshaken faith in God.

Spotting Prahlad in prayer one day
The king asked, "Who do you pray to?"
Unafraid, Prahlad firmly answered,
"To my only true god, Lord Vishnu."

Hiranyakashipu screamed in anger
"Who is greater—your Vishnu or I?"
Prahlad smiled at him calmly,
"Lord Vishnu" was his reply.

The protector of our world,
Is the loving God Vishnu,
In his many forms—his *avatars*
He watches over me and you.

Just like Krishna, Vishnu too
Is the colour of the deep blue sea.
He lives in the heavenly ocean,
With his wife, Goddess Lakshmi.

Vishnu watches over us as he lies
On a snake with a thousand heads,
The divine creature is Sheshnaag
Who serves as his master's bed.

The wicked king Hiranyakashipu
Was so angered by Prahlad's reply,
To make a terrifying example of him
Decided that the boy must die.

He made his men hurl Prahlad
In the path of elephants wild,
It was nothing short of a miracle
That no harm came to the child.

Into a hall crawling with angry snakes
Was the poor Prahlad next thrown,
Yet again he walked out unharmed
By the grace of Lord Vishnu alone.

Evil Holika, whom no fire could harm
Finally decided it was her turn,
To help her brother, she would end
Prahlad's life by making him burn.

With Prahlad in her lap, she sat
On logs of wood used for a pyre,
And laughed wickedly at the boy
As the king's men lit the fire.

Brave Prahlad stayed calm
As he chanted Vishnu's name,
Lo and behold! He was untouched
While Holika perished in the flame.

Why did Holika's magic fail her?
Because her aim was to harm
Only when used to help others,
Does power work like a charm.

Klaka let out a deep breath
The story had him spellbound,
"Amma" he said, "I can hardly wait,
For colourful Holi to come around.

But I have one more question Amma…
What is Holi's *bestest* colour?"
"All colours are beautiful" she said
"Just like every child is to his mother.

Long after Holi has come and gone
And the colours are washed away,
Our endless love for each other
With us will forever and ever stay.

So the colour of love
Is my favourite you see.
As it is the only one
That lasts for eternity."

With those words, Klaka fell asleep.
That night he dreamt happily,
Of playing with Radha and Krishna
The colourful festival of Holi!

Books in the 'Amma Tell Me' Series:

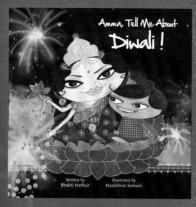

Amma, Tell Me About
Diwali !
Written by Bhakti Mathur
Illustrated by Maulshree Somani

Amma, Tell Me About **Ramayana!**
Written by Bhakti Mathur
Illustrated by Maulshree Somani

Amma, Tell Me About
Krishna !
Written by Bhakti Mathur
Illustrated by Maulshree Somani

Amma, Tell Me
How Krishna Fought the Demons!
Part 2 in the Krishna Trilogy
Written by Bhakti Mathur
Illustrated by Maulshree Somani

Amma, Tell Me
How Krishna Defeated Kansa!
Part 3 in the Krishna Trilogy
Written by Bhakti Mathur
Illustrated by Maulshree Somani

Amma, Tell Me About **Ganesha!**
Written by Bhakti Mathur
Illustrated by Maulshree Somani

Amma, Tell Me About
Hanuman!
Part 1 in the Hanuman Trilogy
Written by
Illustrated by Maulshree Somani

Amma, Tell Me
How Hanuman Crossed the Ocean!
Part 2 in the Hanuman Trilogy
Written by Bhakti Mathur
Illustrated by Maulshree Somani

Amma, Tell Me About
Hanuman's Adventures in Lanka!
Part 3 in the Hanuman Trilogy
Written by
Illustrated by Maulshree Somani

www.bhaktimathur.com

f facebook.com/Ammatellme

🐦 twitter.com/bhaktimathur